NIGHT STORY

Written by
Nancy Willard

Illustrated by
Ilse Plume

Harcourt Brace Jovanovich, Publishers

SAN DIEGO   NEW YORK   LONDON

HBJ

Text copyright ©1981 by Nancy Willard
Illustrations copyright ©1986 by Ilse Plume

Library of Congress Cataloging-in-Publication Data

Willard, Nancy.
Night story.

Summary: A small boy tells about the fantastic events
that may or may not have occurred during
his night's sleep when he took the night train
to the country where nothing lasts.
[1. Night—Fiction.   2. Fantasy]
I. Plume, Ilse, ill.
II. Title.
PZ7.W6553Nh 1986   [E]   85-17677
ISBN 0-15-257348-8

Printed in the United States of America

First edition

A B C D E

For Ariel at bedtime.
Nancy Willard

To Anne-Marie:
Happy Graduation! Vassar '86
Hope your life is filled with
star sprinkles and moonbeams. . . .
Love, Ilse

And I took the night train
to the country where nothing lasts,

and it stopped at the night market
where nothing is sold,
where all is given
and nothing is given for keeps.

And I got some cheese.
And it shone like a blue moon.

And a dream-mouse ate my cheese,
so I kept the mouse,

and a dream-cat ate my mouse,

so I kept the cat,

and a dream-dog chased my cat,
so I kept the dog,

and a dream-wolf chased my dog,
so I kept the wolf,

and a dream-hunter shot my wolf,
so I followed the hunter,

and a dream-horse stole his heart,
so I jumped on behind,
and it carried us both
toward the watchtowers of morning,

and I took the morning train
to my own country,

and it stopped in my own room
where nothing changes,

where the mouse sleeps in its hole
and the cat sleeps on my bed,

where the dog at the door twitches,
dreaming of wolves,

where wolf, hunter, and horse
fold up with the shadows,
and I brought back nothing
except this story.

The illustrations in this book were done in
colored pencil on 140 lb. Strathmore Gemini.

The hand-lettered text type based on
ITC Usherwood was done by Anita Karl.

The display type was set by hand in Shooting Star
by Thompson Type, San Diego, California.

Color separations were made by
Heinz Weber, Inc., Los Angeles, California.

Printed by Holyoke Lithograph,
Springfield, Massachusetts.

Bound by The Book Press,
Brattleboro, Vermont.

Production supervision by
Warren Wallerstein.

Designed by Michael Farmer.